Amelia Bedelia

Cleans Up

☆ Amelia Bedelia
Cleans Up ☆

by Herman Parish

pictures by Lynne Avril

me ♥

Greenwillow Books

An Imprint of HarperCollins Publishers

Gouache and black pencil were used to prepare the black-and-white art.
Amelia Bedelia is a registered trademark of Peppermint Partners, LLC.

Library of Congress Cataloging-in-Publication Data
Parish, Herman.
Amelia Bedelia cleans up / by Herman Parish ; pictures by Lynne Avril.
pages cm—(Amelia Bedelia ; #6)
Summary: "Amelia Bedelia and her friends clean up a vacant lot and build a clubhouse—with surprising results! Includes a guide to idioms used in the book and features black-and-white art throughout"—Provided by publisher.
ISBN 978-0-06-233401-5 (hardback)—ISBN 978-0-06-233400-8 (pbk. ed.)—ISBN 978-0-06-233403-9 (pob)
[1. Clubs—Fiction. 2. Friendship—Fiction. 3. Tree houses—Fiction. 4. Clubhouses—Fiction. 5. Parks—Fiction. 6. Humorous stories.] I. Title. PZ7.P2185Aobg 2015 [E]—dc23 2014032539

15 16 17 18 CG/OPM 10 9 8 7 6 5 4 3 2 1 First Edition

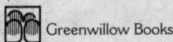 Greenwillow Books

For Dr. Gupta and Dr. Roychowdhury—
thanks a "lot"! —H. P.

For My parents—thank you! —L. A.

Contents

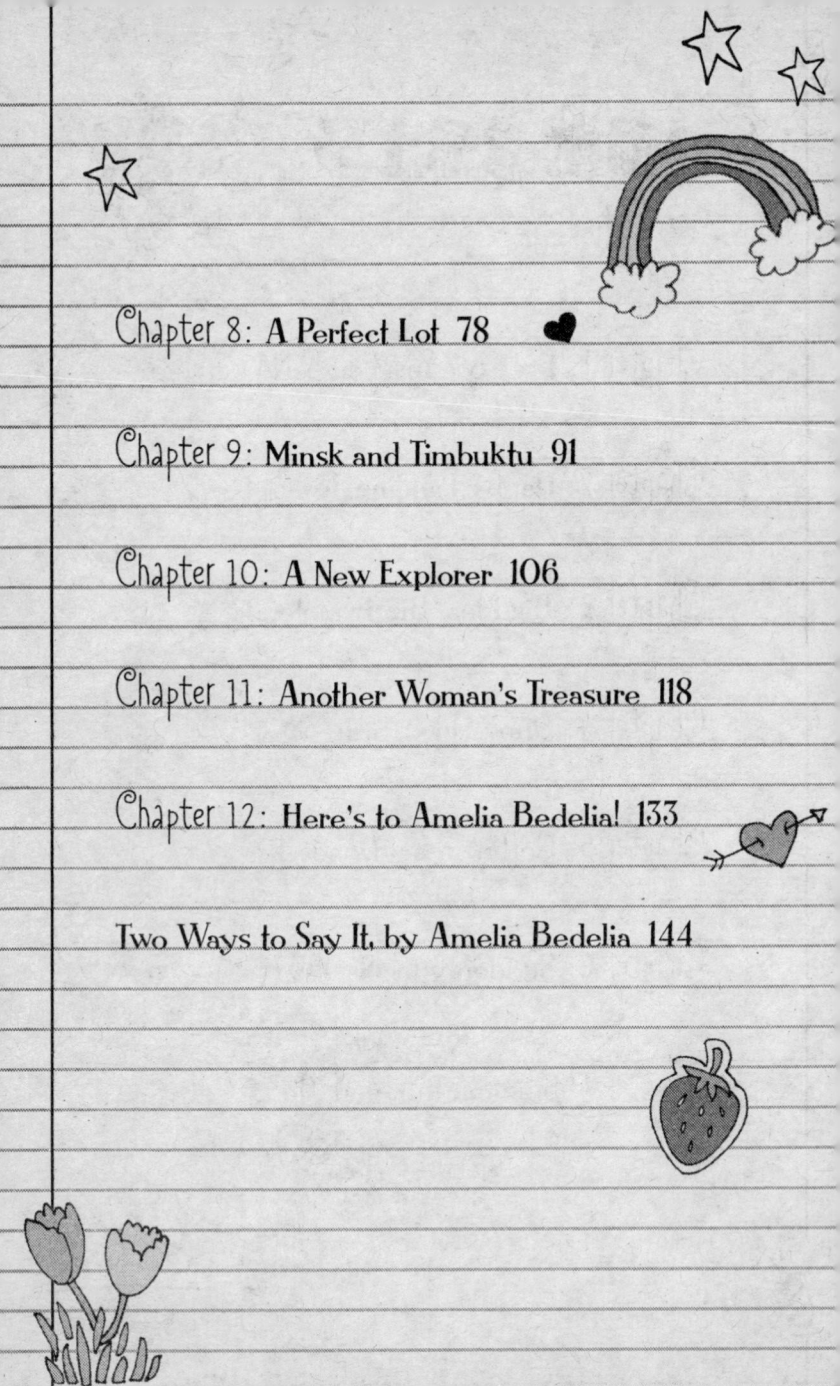

Chapter 1

Breezy? Yes. Easy? No . . .

Amelia Bedelia was as free as a bird. She was pedaling her bike as fast as she could. The wind was blowing in her face and blowing her hair straight back. Now she understood why Finally, her dog, loved to hang her head out the car window on trips.

Amelia Bedelia really wished that every day was this

WOOF! WOOF! WOOF! WOOF!

easy and breezy.
Today she was riding all over town with her friends Holly and Heather. They zipped through the park, zooming past babies in strollers and woofing at the dogs out for a walk. The dogs woofed right back.

"Let's go this way!" shouted Holly.

"Follow me!" yelled Heather.

Amelia Bedelia raced after her friends. As she rode, she imagined changing her

name to Amelia Breezelia, Club President!

She had been the president for about ten minutes. Most clubs come with leaders and followers, with a bunch of rules and regulations. But this club was so new that it didn't even have a name. It had been born in Amelia Bedelia's backyard when Holly and Heather had stopped by an hour earlier.

"I'm bored," Holly had said.

"Me too," said Heather.

"We've got bikes," said Amelia Bedelia. "Let's go exploring. We can start an explorers' club!"

"Not just exploring," said Heather. "Let's have adventures."

"Let's make it our job to have adventures," said Holly.

"Let's start the Explorers' Adventure Club," said Heather.

"How about the Adventuring Explorers' Club?" said Holly.

Amelia Bedelia just wanted to stop talking and get going, so she made a suggestion. "Let's call it Our Club until we come up with a good name. And let's have a rule. One rule."

what rule?

"What rule?" asked Holly.

"No being bored!" said Amelia Bedelia.

"Yes!" said Holly and Heather together.

"That's settled," said Holly. "Now we need to choose a president."

"I vote for me," said Heather.

"I vote for me too!" said Holly.

They turned to Amelia Bedelia to cast the tie-breaking vote.

"You're leaving me no choice," said Amelia Bedelia. "I have to vote for the smartest, prettiest, most adventuresome explorer I know."

Holly and Heather looked at each other. Then they looked back at Amelia Bedelia. Then they asked, "Who?"

"Me!" said Amelia Bedelia.

They all fell over laughing.

"But can we really all be president at the same time?" asked Holly, still giggling.

"We should rotate," said Heather.

"Sure," said Amelia Bedelia. She stood up, turned around in a circle, then sat back down. "My dog does that when she comes into a room and sits."

"I mean," said Heather, "we should take turns."

"Okay, you're next," Amelia Bedelia said.

Holly and Heather stood up, turned in a circle, and sat back down. Then they fell against each other, laughing some more.

Heather stopped giggling long enough to ask, "Where should our club meet?"

"We could meet here, in my backyard," said Amelia Bedelia.

"But we're an explorers' club," said Holly. "We have to get out and see new places!"

"Do new things!" agreed Heather.

"Find a cool clubhouse!" said Amelia Bedelia.

"Yeah!" said Holly. "Where we can relax and hang out."

They all went back to thinking.

Heather and Holly were thinking about where they could build a clubhouse. Amelia Bedelia was wondering what was so relaxing about hanging out laundry.

"Hey," she said, suddenly. "What is our club all about?"

"Having adventures," said Heather.

"Right," said Amelia Bedelia. "So let's have an adventure. Let's go exploring and discover a clubhouse."

No one had to say another word. They

jumped on their bikes, and away they went.

Their adventure took them all over town. But they didn't find any place that seemed just right for a clubhouse. Finally they turned back toward home.

Amelia Bedelia was bringing up the rear as they biked down Pleasant Street, in the oldest neighborhood in town. She slowed down to gaze at the largest house.

It was three stories tall, with skinny windows covered with dark curtains. The paint was peeling, the roof was sagging, and one window on the top floor was cracked. A black cat

sat on the front steps and narrowed yellow eyes at Amelia Bedelia as she rode by.

It looked exactly like a haunted house on a TV show. Amelia Bedelia pedaled faster to get past it and catch up with Holly and Heather.

Her two friends were way ahead, about to turn left. Next to the spooky house was a large vacant lot with an enormous oak tree in the center.

Holly and Heather disappeared around the corner. That was when Amelia Bedelia made an adventurous decision.

Making a sharp left too, she jumped the curb and headed straight into the vacant lot to cut across it diagonally. If she raced through the lot, she could

catch up with Holly and Heather.

It was tough to keep her bike rolling over lumpy dirt and knee-high grass. But Amelia Bedelia just pedaled harder. In a few seconds, she would burst out of the bushes ahead of Heather and Holly.

Just as she stood up on her pedals to go as fast as possible, her front tire wedged

11

between a rock and a branch. The front wheel of her bike stopped, but her back wheel kept on going. So did Amelia Bedelia, sailing over her handlebars.

She felt the wind rushing past her ears. Time seemed to slow down, as if she were watching herself in slow motion, soaring free as a bird. Flying upside down certainly was breezy, she thought. But Amelia Bedelia knew that her landing was not going to be easy.

Chapter 2

Happy Landing

Amelia Bedelia rolled over and opened her eyes. She was lying flat on her back. Out of her right eye, she saw a bright blue sky. Her left eye was looking up into an enormous canopy of green leaves. She had flown for just a few seconds, but here she was looking at the same thing every bird looks at every day—blue sky

to soar through
and branches to rest on.

She checked herself over
to see if anything was broken.

She knew that her two eyes still worked. She lifted her right arm and then her left arm. Okay so far. She lifted her left leg and then her right one. Check. Slowly she sat up and looked around. She was in much better shape than her bike.

Her bike was busted. The front wheel was twisted into something like a figure eight.

"Amelia Bedelia?" shouted Heather.

"Amelia Bedelia!" yelled Holly.

She could hear them, so Amelia Bedelia figured that her ears must be okay too. She answered, "Over here!"

Heather and Holly dropped their bikes on the sidewalk and came running through the empty lot. When they saw Amelia Bedelia next to her crunched bike, they hurried to kneel down beside her.

"Are you okay?" said Holly.

"Why did you ride through this junky lot?" Heather asked.

"I was trying to take a shortcut," answered Amelia Bedelia. She looked at her left knee. It was scraped. She looked at her right elbow. It was bloody. "Only I'm the one who got cut," she added. "From now on, I'm taking only long cuts." Maybe that didn't sound very adventurous, but it would be safer.

"We would have waited for you," said Heather.

"You're lucky you didn't get really hurt," said Holly. "You could have landed on this!" She held up something that looked like a giant rusty corkscrew.

"Or that!" said Heather. She pointed

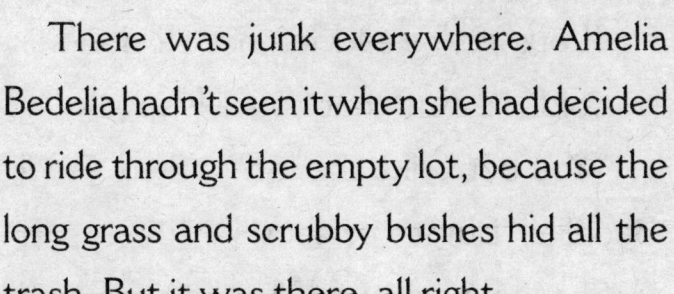

to a board with nails in it.

There was junk everywhere. Amelia Bedelia hadn't seen it when she had decided to ride through the empty lot, because the long grass and scrubby bushes hid all the trash. But it was there, all right.

"Yikes," said Holly. "Maybe adventure isn't all it's cracked up to be."

"My bike helmet isn't cracked either," said Amelia Bedelia. She took it off and patted it affectionately. "I'm glad I had it on."

Holly helped Amelia Bedelia get to her feet.

Amelia Bedelia hopped a few steps and decided that her sore knee was not too bad. She could walk on it. And that was good, because it looked like she would

have to walk home.

"Let's go," said Heather. "I don't like this old lot. And that house is spooky."

"You don't like the lot?" asked Amelia Bedelia. "But it's perfect!"

She looked around. So did her friends. They saw:

Tall grass.

Big rocks.

Broken bricks.

Crumbling cinder blocks.

Empty cans.

Bits of metal.

Twists of wire.

Old tires.

Falling-apart chairs.

And a giant oak tree.

Amelia Bedelia limped to the tree. The trunk was so wide her arms could not reach all the way around it. It was so tall that it rose above the houses on either side of the lot. The leaves and branches were so thick that when Amelia Bedelia tipped her head back, she could not see the sky.

"Perfect?" asked Holly. "Perfect for what?"

"For our new clubhouse!" said Amelia Bedelia. "Our explorers' clubhouse!"

Heather looked at Holly. Holly looked at Heather. Heather and Holly both looked at Amelia Bedelia.

"Maybe you'd better sit back down," said Holly. "I think you might have hit your head harder than you thought. Are

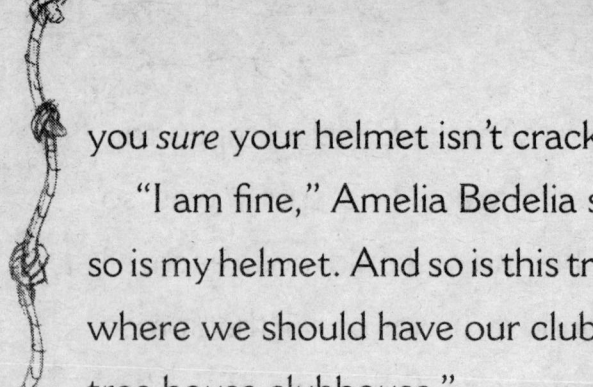

you *sure* your helmet isn't cracked?"

"I am fine," Amelia Bedelia said. "And so is my helmet. And so is this tree! This is where we should have our clubhouse—a tree house clubhouse."

Holly looked up. So did Heather. Holly started to grin. So did Heather.

"We could get up and down with a ladder," said Holly.

"How about climbing a rope?" said Amelia Bedelia.

"A rope ladder," said Heather.

"Great," said Holly. "We could pull it up after us and be completely on our own. Like we were on a desert island!"

"We could have windows," said Heather.

"A telescope," said Holly. "So we can

see what's happening all over town."

"A hammock!" said Heather. "So we can lie in the sun."

"A roof," said Holly. "So we can rest in the shade."

"A slide for getting down!" said Heather.

"Or a pole for sliding down!" said Holly.

"It's perfect!" said Heather. "Even though you found it by accident, Amelia Bedelia."

"It wasn't that bad an accident," said Amelia Bedelia, rubbing her sore elbow. "And it was totally worth it."

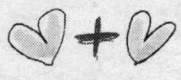

Chapter 3

Big Idea, Big Trouble

At dinnertime, Amelia Bedelia let her parents in on her idea. *She* could tell that it was a great idea by how much she was waving her arms around as she told them all about the new club, the vacant lot, and the plans for a tree house. Waving arms always meant that

22

something exciting was about to happen.

But for her parents, Amelia Bedelia's waving arms were a warning, setting off alarm bells, buzzers, and whistles.

"We'll have a rope ladder to get up into the tree house!" Amelia Bedelia said. "We'll have a telescope and windows and a hammock and a balcony! Won't it be great?" She took a big bite of her chicken drumstick and beamed at her mom and dad.

"Well, sweetness," said her mother, "I must say . . ."

But she didn't say anything. She looked over at her husband, and she arched her

23

right eyebrow in secret parent code. Then she added, "This plan sounds . . . What's the word I'm searching for, honey?"

Amelia Bedelia's father put his fork down. "Unbelievable," he said.

"I knew you'd like it!" said Amelia Bedelia. "It's perfect for us!"

Her father tilted his head so he could look right at her. "Of all the dangerous, hazardous, perilous—"

Amelia Bedelia kept hearing "us" at the end of every word. She interrupted him.

"When I said 'us,' I didn't mean you and me and Mom. Us three girls can handle it."

"Ridiculous!" said her father. "You girls are not

Ridiculous
hazardous!

24

ngerous! ridiculous! ...lous!

hazardous! treacherous!

perilous!

ridiculous!

treacherous!

going to handle anything in that empty lot!" said her father.

"It's not empty," explained Amelia Bedelia. "It's full of trash and stuff."

"Exactly!" said her father.

"Honey," said Amelia Bedelia's mother, "your dad does not think this is a good idea at all, and I don't think you're going to convince him. You're banging your head against a stone wall here."

"I didn't bang my head on anything," said Amelia Bedelia. "Just my elbow and my knee, and I banged them on the ground, not a wall."

"You banged your knee?" her father asked. "You banged your elbow? How? Where? What happened?"

Amelia Bedelia stood up to show off the scrapes on her elbow and knee, and explained how she had done a somersault over her bike.

"Treacherous!" exclaimed her father.

Amelia Bedelia sat down again. She was beginning to get the idea that "us" words were not the friends of explorers. Except, of course, for "adventurous."

"Honey," said her mother, "your dad is right. That lot is no place for children to play. Look what happened to you already. It's not safe."

"I know," agreed Amelia Bedelia. "That's why we have to clean it up!"

Amelia Bedelia could see that her parents still didn't understand. So she followed her number-one rule: she turned to her mother and asked a question.

"Aren't you always telling me we need a sense of community? To give something back to where we are?"

Her mother's eyebrows went up.

"Pleasant Street is just a couple of

blocks away. Isn't that our community?"

Her mother's eyebrows made two tall arches. Her father put his elbows on the table and leaned his forehead on his hands. He sighed.

This, thought Amelia Bedelia, was progress. Time for one more question. "Can't we give back by taking away? Collecting all that junk and recycling and getting rid of the rest?"

Her father sighed again.

"We need to think about this for a minute," Amelia Bedelia's mother said. "Any more questions?"

"Yes," Amelia Bedelia said. "Would you please pass the kale?"

She knew that question would make

her mother happy. Every time her mother served them kale, Amelia Bedelia and her father got a lecture about why it was so good for you, along with a helping of the dark green leaves.

Smiling, her mother passed the kale and watched in delight as Amelia Bedelia piled it on her plate. Her father watched carefully. The more kale Amelia Bedelia ate, the less there would be for him.

Amelia Bedelia chewed and chewed.

She tried not to think about what she was eating or how it tasted. Her parents had stopped eating altogether and were staring at each other. They must have been saying things in secret parent code that Amelia Bedelia had not yet worked out, because suddenly her mom spoke.

"All right," said her mother. "You and your friends can clean up that lot. I don't know who owns it, but whoever it is, they haven't done anything with it in years. I'm sure they won't mind if the trash gets taken away. But grown-ups have to be there with you." Then she turned to Amelia Bedelia's father and said, "Honey, I'm sure you wouldn't mind giving up your golf tournament this Saturday to help our

daughter give back to our community, right?"

Amelia Bedelia's father closed his eyes and made a face. He looked as if the idea of giving up his golf game was even more bitter than kale.

"Sweetie, you're asking a whole lot," he said to Amelia Bedelia.

"Of course," Amelia Bedelia agreed. "It wouldn't be any good to clean up just part of the lot. But don't worry. With everyone working together, I'm sure we can clean it up in no time!"

Chapter 4

One Man's Trash

On Saturday morning, Amelia Bedelia and her parents loaded rakes and shovels, clippers and recycling bins into their car.

First they stopped by a hardware store to get bags for the trash and gloves to protect their hands. "You come back, now!" the clerk called as they walked out the door.

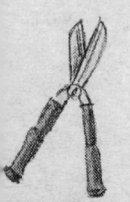

"Okay," said Amelia Bedelia. She turned around and headed right back into the store. "Why did you want me to come back?" she asked the clerk. "Did we forget something?"

"Never mind, sweetie," her mother said, coming after her. "Let's get to work!"

They drove to the empty lot. Once they arrived and had unloaded all of their equipment, Amelia Bedelia took a look at her parents in their boots and flannel shirts. Her dad was wearing a hat. Her mom had a bandanna around her neck. Amelia Bedelia looked at herself. She had a flannel shirt and a hat.

"We look like lumberjacks," her father said.

"Could Mom and I be lumberjills?" Amelia Bedelia asked.

Her mom laughed. "We can be anything we want, since we're working hard!" she said. "Here's the plan. Dad and I will move big things to the side of the lot. Tomorrow Heather and Holly and their parents will come by with a pickup truck and haul stuff to the dump. Amelia Bedelia, you're in charge of picking up litter. Let's get to it!"

The first thing Amelia Bedelia's parents found was an old refrigerator.

"Cool!" said Amelia Bedelia.

"Not so cool," said her father as he staggered past her with it. Sweat was dripping down his face.

Amelia Bedelia picked up clumps of newspaper, sneakers without laces, and empty cans and bottles. She stuffed the trash into bags and dumped the paper

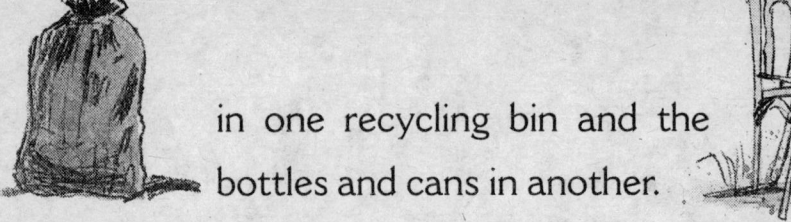

in one recycling bin and the bottles and cans in another.

"I'll take that," said her father, reaching out through the broken screen of an old TV and grabbing one of her cans. "I'm glad you brought this in today. How long has it been in your family?"

Amelia Bedelia knew he was pretending to be on his favorite TV show, the one where people brought in junk from the attic and hoped to be told it was worth a million dollars. "About a minute," she told him.

"Well, it's certainly in great condition," her father continued. "It still has the label.

Will you read it for our audience, please?"

"'Grape juice,'" read Amelia Bedelia.

"Right you are," her father said. "This is a spectacular squashed grape juice can. It's priceless! Congratulations!"

"Get the lead out, you two!" called Amelia Bedelia's mother.

"Oh, no, did you find some lead?" Amelia Bedelia asked.

"She means keep working," explained her father. "We're not done."

Her parents cleared away a smelly mattress and a bookcase  warped from the rain. Amelia Bedelia found tires. A lot of tires. At least twelve of them. "I'm tired of tires." She sighed.

"Ah," said her father. "That's because you haven't yet been introduced to the fabulous new game of tire bowling."

He set one of the tires on its edge and gave it a big push. It rolled and wobbled toward the end of the lot, bumped into the old refrigerator, and fell over with a *thump*.

"Strike!" he yelled.

Amelia Bedelia hit another tire with her fist.

"No, don't hit. See if you can roll the tire and hit the refrigerator," he said. She did. Pretty soon all the tires were

over on the other end of the lot.

"Wow, look at that pile of junk," he said. "This lot has everything but the kitchen sink!"

"Dad? What's this?" called Amelia Bedelia. She was poking a stick at something behind a scrubby bush.

"Never mind," said her father, coming to look over her shoulder. "That's a kitchen sink."

They carried the kitchen sink over to their junk pile. Amelia Bedelia's mother was already there, leaning against the refrigerator. Amelia Bedelia and her father flopped down for a rest too, and her mom handed them big bottles of

water, which they guzzled down.

"I think that's enough for one day," Amelia Bedelia's mom said.

They loaded the bags of trash and the recycling bins into the car and got ready to go. Amelia Bedelia ran back to give the oak tree a hug and a pat. "We'll be back soon," she whispered to it.

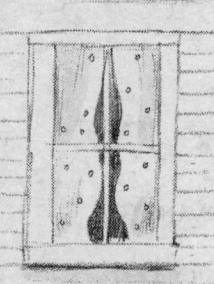

She was facing the spooky old house next to the lot, and she thought she saw movement in one of the windows. A curtain fluttered, as if somebody had lifted it and then dropped it again.

Was somebody at home? And was that person watching them?

Chapter 5
Getting a Lot Done

The next day Amelia Bedelia's family drove back to the lot. Heather and Holly were already there with their parents, and a pickup truck was parked at the curb.

"We'll take the refrigerator first," Heather's dad said.

The three girls left the grown-ups talking and wandered away, looking at

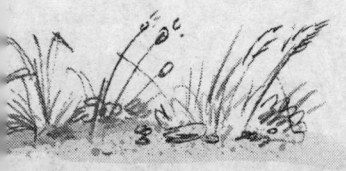

their lot. The grass was still high and the weeds were still everywhere, but it didn't look quite as messy as it had before.

"Look! There's a cat!" Holly called out, pointing to a bush.

Amelia Bedelia saw a flash of fluffy gray fur among the leaves.

"We're going to mow the grass around that bush," she said. "I hope the cat doesn't run out and get hurt."

Heather looked worried.

"Maybe we should get it to go away."

"How?" Holly asked.

"Here, kitty!" called Heather.

Amelia Bedelia stuck a hand in the bush, trying to reach the cat's collar. But the cat hissed a warning at her.

Amelia Bedelia grabbed one of the branches. She shook the bush lightly. The cat didn't move. Then Holly shook the bush, and Heather smacked the bush with

a stick, rustling all the leaves. The cat rushed out, darted between Amelia Bedelia's legs, and scampered away.

"Let's get started," Amelia Bedelia's mom called out. "Girls, that goes for you too. No more beating around the bush."

"We're finished," Amelia Bedelia said. "We were just beating the bush to get a cat to run out."

"What?" asked her mother. "Never mind. Grab gloves and let's get to work!"

Heather, Holly, and Amelia Bedelia finished picking up the trash. The three dads made trips to the dump while the three moms mowed the grass and the girls pulled weeds and trimmed bushes.

When the dads returned in the

pickup truck, they were very impressed. "This is great," said Holly's father. "I think we can call it a day."

"Why should we call it a day?" asked Amelia Bedelia. "It's a lot."

"I know," he said. "And it looks good."

"It sure does." Holly nodded. "We got a lot done."

"That's what we came here to do," Amelia Bedelia agreed happily.

The lot *did* look great. It would be a wonderful place to build an explorers' clubhouse. The oak tree rose out of a square of smooth grass. There was no trash to be seen anywhere. There were

only a few weeds left to be pulled.

"Let's come back next weekend and finish weeding," said Holly. She and Heather and Amelia Bedelia flopped down under the oak tree to rest.

"Girls!" called Holly's mother. "We're making one last trip to the dump. Do you want to ride with us or walk home?"

"Walk!" all three girls called back. They relaxed for a while longer, looking up.

Amelia Bedelia wished she could be in the tree right now, swaying back and forth as the wind rocked the strong, thick branches and rustled the dark green leaves. Being in a tree house would really be easy and breezy, she thought. It would be just like being a bird.

"Pretty soon we'll be able to break ground on our tree house!" said Heather.

"Don't you mean break branch?" asked Holly, and she giggled.

"But if the branches break, our tree house will fall down!" Amelia Bedelia was worried. "We don't want that to happen. Like that lullaby where the cradle falls

out of the tree. I always think that's a scary thing to sing to a little baby!"

"Don't worry, Amelia Bedelia," Heather said. "I'm sure no cradles really fall out of trees, and I'm sure our tree house will be very safe too. Let's go get a snack. I'm starving!"

"We can go to Pete's Diner on the way home," Amelia Bedelia said.

The girls got up and walked toward Pete's, thinking of cool milk shakes, hot, crispy french fries, and chocolaty brownies. Amelia Bedelia's stomach rumbled so loudly that a man walking past on the sidewalk turned to look at her.

"Well, bless my bluebottles, if it isn't

little Miss Amelia Bedelia!" he exclaimed. Amelia Bedelia recognized him right away. It was easy because he was the only person she knew who wore a ten-gallon hat, like a cowboy, everywhere he went. His name was Wild Bill, and he owned a used car lot on the other side of town.

"How are you, Mr. Bill?" she asked politely.

"Mighty fine, little lady. You

look like you've been hard at work. What have you been up to these days?"

"A lot," said Amelia Bedelia.

Wild Bill looked alarmed. "Not Lots of Lemons again!" he exclaimed.

Amelia Bedelia remembered the lemonade stand she had set up right outside Wild Bill's Auto-Rama. Since she squeezed the juice of one whole lemon into every glass, she made a sign that read LOTS OF LEMONS! Wild Bill had not been happy about that. Amelia Bedelia didn't know that some people used the word "lemon" to mean a used car that didn't work well!

"No, nothing to do with cars," she promised Wild Bill. "My friends and I are

cleaning up a vacant lot.
We're going to build
a clubhouse in a tree."

Wild Bill shook his
head. "If you can pull that
off, just the three of you, I'll eat
my hat!"

"I don't think it would taste
very good," said Amelia Bedelia,
but Wild Bill didn't hear her. He waved
good-bye and went on his way, chuckling
to himself.

The girls reached Pete's and stepped
into the diner. "Amelia Bedelia!" Pete
called out. "Long time no see!"

"That's terrible!" said Amelia Bedelia.
She waved her hand in front of Pete's

face. "What happened to your eyes?"

"My eyes are fine," said Pete. "Just come in and sit down here at the counter and chew the fat! I haven't seen you in a while."

Amelia Bedelia and her friends hopped onto the tall stools at the counter. But Amelia Bedelia hoped that Pete would not actually serve her a plate of fat. Yuck! She'd rather eat french fries any day.

"Milk shakes, please," said Holly.

"I'd like strawberry," said Amelia Bedelia.

"Vanilla!" said Heather.

"Chocolate!" said Holly.

Doris, Amelia Bedelia's favorite waitress, whipped up the milk shakes and brought over three tall glasses. "What have you been up to?" she asked Amelia Bedelia.

"A lot," said Amelia Bedelia.

"I can imagine," said Doris. "You're a good worker. I still remember when you were a waitress in training here. So what's been keeping you so busy?"

"A whole lot," said Amelia Bedelia. "We cleaned up the empty lot on Pleasant Street."

"Good thing you're cleaning up that place. It's an eyesore!" Pete called over from the grill.

"You're right! My eyes got really sore from all the dirt and dust," said Amelia Bedelia, rubbing them.

Pete shook his head and flipped a hamburger, smiling.

"We're going to build a tree house," Holly said.

"And meet in it to talk about what *other* adventures we'd like to have!" Amelia Bedelia added.

"Like skydiving over the Grand Canyon!" said Heather.

"Or scuba diving on the Great Barrier Reef," said Holly.

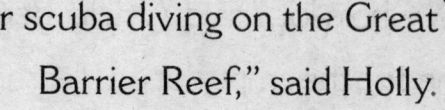

"What would be your best adventure, Amelia Bedelia?" Heather asked.

Amelia Bedelia thought about it. What would she do? She would take an airplane anywhere she wanted. Flying on an airplane wasn't really as easy and breezy as flying like a bird, but she wouldn't mind. She could pat the nose of the Great Sphinx. She could climb up a zigzaggy pyramid in the jungles of Central America, and swing through the trees with monkeys and macaws. She could ride a scooter through the streets of Rome. Now *that* would feel easy and breezy.

"Come on, Amelia Bedelia," Heather urged. "Tell us!"

"I want to go around the world," Amelia Bedelia said. She sucked up the last of her milk shake, letting her straw make loud slurping noises. "That way I never have to stop exploring!"

Heather and Holly finished up their milk shakes too. "We'd better get going," Holly said, jumping down. "Our parents will be wondering where we are."

The girls paid their bill, said good-bye to Pete and Doris, and headed home.

Chapter 6

Suddenly for Sale

Amelia Bedelia slept late the next Saturday, with Finally snuggled up on her bed.

After lunch she hurried to the empty lot. Heather and Holly were there, standing next to a big new sign. It hadn't been there last weekend—Amelia Bedelia was sure of that.

Amelia Bedelia waved from across the street.

"Hi!" she hollered. But Heather and Holly did not wave back. When she reached them, Amelia Bedelia saw why.

A big red sign said FOR SALE in bright white letters.

"For sale?" gasped Amelia Bedelia. "Our lot is for sale?"

 "It isn't ours, really," said Holly miserably. "I guess whoever owns it decided it was time to sell it."

"But now we can't build a tree house here." Heather sighed. After all their hard work! It really didn't seem fair.

"I wish we could buy the lot ourselves," said Holly. "How much do you think it would cost? It's just dirt and grass and stuff."

"And our tree," said Amelia Bedelia,

patting the oak tree gently. "I get three dollars a week for my allowance."

Heather and Holly each got two dollars and fifty cents. "If we put it all together, could we buy the lot?" Holly asked.

The three friends were not sure. But they didn't feel like pulling up weeds anymore. What would be the point?

"Let's go to Pete's," said Amelia Bedelia. "It might make us feel better."

"Back for another round of milk shakes, girls?" asked Doris. Then she saw their sad faces. "Wow," she said. "You look down in the mouth!"

Amelia Bedelia knew this was true. She could feel the corners of her mouth

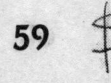

dragging down in a frown.

Doris whipped up a thick, frothy milk shake with extra chocolate and poured it into a glass. She'd made so much that a little spilled over the lip of the glass and onto the counter. "Whoops!" she said, sticking three straws into the icy drink and setting it down in front of Heather, Holly, and Amelia Bedelia. "This one's on me," she told them, wiping up the spill. "What's wrong?"

"I think the milk shake is really on the

counter," Amelia Bedelia
said. "Don't worry; you
didn't get any on you. But
what's wrong is that somebody's selling
our lot—the one we've been cleaning up
for our tree house."

Pete came over and listened as Amelia
Bedelia explained about finding the FOR
SALE sign. He shook his head. "That's a
tough break," he said. "You girls really got
the rug pulled out from under you."

"Oh, we didn't have any rugs yet,"
said Amelia Bedelia.
"We hadn't even started
on our tree house. But we
were almost ready to start."

"Maybe we'll be able

to buy the lot ourselves!" Holly said hopefully. "We thought if we put all our allowances together, we might be able to."

"Hmm," said Pete. "I don't know about that. But if I had any questions about buying and selling some land, there's the person I'd ask."

He pointed to a lady sitting in a booth. She was talking on a cell phone and had a laptop on the table in front of her.

"That's Jill," Pete said. "She's an old friend of mine, and she's a real estate agent—she helps people buy and sell houses and land and things like that."

"Things like our lot?" Amelia Bedelia asked excitedly.

"Just like your lot," said Pete. "You

can ask Jill anything you'd like. She's a good person; she'd give you the shirt off her back."

"I don't think it would fit me very well," said Amelia Bedelia. She hopped off the stool and went over to Jill's booth, followed by Holly and Heather, just as Jill finished her call.

Pete introduced her to the three girls. "They've got some questions about real estate," he said, "and I told them you would be able to help."

"Is there such a thing as fake estate?" Amelia Bedelia asked, surprised.

Jill was wearing a bright green shirt. It was a pretty color even if it wouldn't fit a girl, thought Amelia Bedelia. But she still hoped that Jill would not give it to her. That would be embarrassing! Jill also had swinging earrings in her ears and lots of rings on her fingers.

"Well, real estate is just what we call houses or other buildings or land," Jill said cheerfully. "I suppose if somebody tried to sell a house or some land that they didn't really own or that doesn't actually exist, that could be fake estate. But nobody would try a stunt like that with

me! I wasn't born yesterday, you know!"

"Oh, yes, I could tell that," said Amelia Bedelia. "I can tell you were born years ago."

"Okay, that's enough!" Jill laughed, which made her earrings swing. "What did you girls want to know?"

They explained about the lot, and Heather asked how much it would cost to buy it. "I can't say for sure," Jill told them. "That's a nice neighborhood. Lots

probably sell at two-fifty, maybe three."

"Great," said Amelia Bedelia. "Holly and Heather both get two-fifty and I get three every week—"

"You do?" said Jill. "You get three hundred thousand dollars every week?"

"Hundred?" asked Holly.

"Thousand?" asked Heather.

"How long would we have to save up our allowances to get just one thousand dollars?" Amelia Bedelia asked her friends.

$$\$2.^{50} + \$2.^{50} + \$3.^{00} = \$8.^{00} \times 1 \ year =$$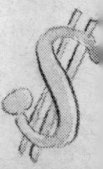

"Yikes!" Holly said. "Two-fifty plus two-fifty plus three . . . that's eight dollars a week. If we saved up for a year . . . um . . ."

Jill picked up a calculator. "If you saved

up for a year, you'd have four hundred and twenty-four dollars among you," she said. "I don't think that would be enough to buy your vacant lot."

"Can we do anything else?" asked Holly. "We really wanted that tree house."

"Do you know the name of the realtor who's selling the lot?" Jill asked.

"It was on the sign," Amelia Bedelia said. "I remember. Victor Lee."

"Oh, I know Victor!" Jill said. "I will keep an ear out, girls. And if I hear anything, I'll let you know."

Jill tucked her hair behind her ear as she said that, so Amelia Bedelia knew she'd keep her promise.

Chapter 7

Stuck in the Mud

All week in school, Amelia Bedelia thought about adventures. In her mind, she rappelled down Mount Everest and sailed around Cape Horn.

"Where are you, Amelia Bedelia?" her teacher asked. "You're a million miles away."

"My body is right here in the classroom, Mrs. Shauk," said Amelia Bedelia. "But

my brain is going around the world."

"Good thing," said Mrs. Shauk. "Because I'd like your brain to help out with our geography lesson, please. Can you come up to the map and show the class where the Pacific Ocean is?"

That was easy for Amelia Bedelia. But it wasn't so easy to think that their explorers' club would no longer have the perfect easy, breezy place to meet.

The next weekend, she and Holly and

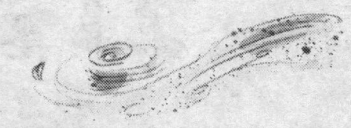

Heather agreed to visit the lot one last time and say good-bye to their oak tree. It rained overnight, but the sun came out in the morning, and Amelia Bedelia set out for the lot, carrying a basket.

When she got there, she saw Holly and Heather sitting sadly by the FOR SALE sign. "What's in the basket, Amelia Bedelia?" asked Holly.

"Lemon tarts!" said Amelia Bedelia. "I baked them this morning."

Amelia Bedelia's lemon tarts were

definitely tart. And also sweet and crunchy and tasty.

"These are really good, Amelia Bedelia," said Holly, munching. "Do you still sell them to Pete for his diner?"

"Sure," said Amelia Bedelia. "I make him a batch every week."

The tarts were delicious, but they were not quite enough to cheer up the girls.

"Amelia Bedelia!" called a loud voice.

Amelia looked up to see her friend Diana strolling by on the sidewalk. Diana was walking five dogs.

"Quick, put the tarts in the basket!" said Amelia Bedelia. She knew how much the dogs that Diana walked for her dog-walking business loved lemon tarts.

There was Sherlock, the bloodhound, with his sad eyes and floppy ears; Dempsey, the boxer, with his blunt nose; Lincoln, the bearded collie, trotting politely by Diana's side; and Snowdrift, the husky, pulling at her leash. There was also a new dog in the pack that Amelia Bedelia had not met before. She was very little, very furry, and black as midnight.

Diana told the dogs to sit, and they sat—except for the new one. That one ran straight to Amelia Bedelia and began sniffing her knees and licking her toes.

"That's Licorice," said Diana. "She's just a puppy, and she isn't doing too well with her training, I'm afraid. She's so friendly that she never wants to sit or stay when there are people to greet!"

"She's sweet!" said Holly, scratching behind Licorice's ears. "Can we play with her? That would cheer us up."

"Sure," said Diana. "But why do you need to be cheered up?"

While Holly and Amelia Bedelia ran around the empty lot with Licorice,

Heather explained to Diana about the tree house they were no longer going to have. Amelia Bedelia, meanwhile, was discovering that playing with a puppy is the perfect way to feel better.

Licorice pounced on sticks and shook them fiercely in her mouth. She chased her tail and yipped with surprise when she caught it. Then she chased Holly. Then she chased Amelia Bedelia. Then she smelled something interesting in a bush. She stopped to sniff— and pulled her leash right out of Amelia Bedelia's hand.

A sleek black cat leaped out
of the bush. The puppy was so surprised
that she tumbled over backward.

The cat dashed for the oak tree.
Licorice dashed after the cat. And Amelia
Bedelia dashed after Licorice.

Amelia Bedelia ran so fast that she
forgot to look where she was going. She
stepped into a patch of mud, slipped, and
flopped down on the seat of her pants.

The cat had scrambled up the oak tree,

but Licorice had already forgotten all about it. She ran back to Amelia Bedelia and bounced into her lap, licking her face and wagging her tail so hard that more mud splattered on Amelia Bedelia. Mud splattered all over Heather and Holly too, when they came running to help Amelia Bedelia up.

"Oh, no!" said Diana. She dropped the leashes for Lincoln, Dempsey, Sherlock, and Snowdrift and hurried over. "I'm so sorry, Amelia Bedelia. Don't tell anybody that the dog I'm supposed to be training got all

three of you so dirty. My name will be mud!"

"My pants are mud too!" said Amelia Bedelia.

While Amelia Bedelia was brushing off some of the mud, and while Diana was getting hold of Licorice's leash, a car pulled up next to the lot. Two men got out. One was wearing a baseball cap and jeans. The other was wearing a suit and tie and carrying a clipboard.

"So, Mr. Lee," said the man in the baseball cap, "this is the lot you wanted to show me?"

Chapter 8

A Perfect Lot

"This is it!" said the man in the suit. "Perfect for any kind of development."

Amelia Bedelia looked at Heather and Holly. Heather and Holly looked at Amelia Bedelia.

"It's him!" whispered Heather.

"It's Victor Lee! He's the one who's going to sell our lot!"

"Looks good," said the man in the baseball cap. "Plenty of room to put up a new building. A parking lot too. And a nice neighborhood. I think this would be an excellent place for my dry cleaning business!"

Diana picked up Licorice. Just as she did so, Lincoln, the collie, spotted the black cat that Licorice had chased up the tree. He raced off to run around the oak tree and bark and bark at the cat. The

WOOF!

other four grown-up dogs joined him. The cat sat on the branch and stared down at the dogs.

WOOF!

WOOF!
WOOF!

WOOF! WOOF!

WOOF!

"I'm sure it will be perfect," said Victor Lee, raising his voice a little over the barking. "Girls? Excuse me? Do you live in this neighborhood?"

"Yes, we do," said Amelia Bedelia. She and Heather and Holly walked over to where the men were standing.

"Don't you think this neighborhood needs a dry cleaner?" Victor Lee asked hopefully.

"I don't know," said Amelia Bedelia. "I usually wash stuff that I want clean. How can you clean things by drying them?"

But the man in the baseball cap was looking at the three girls and frowning.

"You girls live around here?" he asked. "You sure?"

"Of course we're sure!" said Heather. "We know where we live!"

"Then this lot would not be perfect after all," the man in the baseball cap said firmly. "Why would I open a dry cleaning business in this neighborhood if people go around looking like that?"

He waved a hand at the three muddy girls. Victor Lee looked dismayed.

"No, thank you, Mr. Lee," said the man in the baseball cap. "If you think I'm going to spend money on this lot, you're barking up the wrong tree!"

"I think it's the dogs who are barking," Amelia Bedelia told him. "And it's the right tree. It has the cat in it."

The man shook his head and marched back to the car. Victor Lee looked at the three girls, shook his head too, and drove away. Diana collected her dogs, waved good-bye, and went on with her walk. Amelia Bedelia, Heather, and Holly sat down to finish their lemon tarts.

"That's not the same cat we saw before, is it?" asked Heather.

"No, it's a different one," said Holly. "Do you think it's okay? Can it get down?"

"When it's ready, it will," said Amelia Bedelia. "But maybe we can help it get ready."

She broke off a small piece of lemon tart. She left it at the foot of the tree.

"Lucky cat," said Heather, licking her fingers. "I wish I could have another."

"You can!" said Amelia Bedelia. "I made a bunch!" She handed out more tarts. And they were just beginning to eat

them when Victor Lee pulled up again.

He got out of his car and frowned when he saw the girls. "Do you girls play in this lot a lot?" he asked. "Are you planning to go home anytime soon?"

A woman got out of the car and came

to stand by Victor. "Wow, those sure smell good," she said. "What are you girls eating?"

"Lemon tarts," said Amelia Bedelia. "Would you like a taste?" She broke off

half of her lemon tart and offered it to the woman.

The woman took a bite. Her eyes went wide, and she shivered a little. "Oh, my!" she said. "That is one tart tart! Did you buy it somewhere around here?"

"No, I made it," said Amelia Bedelia. "But if you want to buy one, I make them for Pete's Diner every week."

"You do?" said the woman. She looked worried for some reason. "Is Pete's Diner near here?"

"Yes," Amelia Bedelia said helpfully. "It's right around the corner. He has wonderful brownies too."

"And milk shakes," added Heather. "The best in town."

"Oh!" the woman said. "That's terrible!"

"How can milk shakes be terrible?" asked Holly.

"Or brownies," added Heather.

"I was planning to open a bakery on this lot," said the woman. "But I don't think anyone would come to it if they can get lemon tarts like these nearby."

"People in this neighborhood really like Pete's Diner," Amelia Bedelia agreed.

The woman looked discouraged. "Mr. Lee, do you have any other lots you could show me?"

She turned back to the car. Victor Lee looked down at the girls. "Do you think you could try not to talk to my clients anymore?" he asked.

Victor Lee and the bakery woman drove away, and the girls finished their tarts. The black cat watched them eat. Then it slowly climbed down the tree and nibbled at the bit of lemon tart that Amelia Bedelia had left on the moss.

"Good kitty!" said Amelia Bedelia. The cat washed its whiskers and trotted through the grass toward the spooky house next door, just as Victor Lee pulled up in his car again! He sighed when he got out and saw that the girls were still sitting by the FOR SALE sign.

This time a man got out of the passenger side of the car. He was wearing a shirt with bright red-and-green parrots on it, and when he spoke, his voice was a little like a parrot's too—harsh and loud.

"This is great!" he said. "This is perfect! This is exactly what I needed!"

Amelia Bedelia exchanged a worried glance with Holly and Heather.

"Excuse me, sir," Amelia Bedelia said. "But we think the lot is perfect too. We like it just the way it is. What are you planning to do to it?"

The man waved his arms.

"I'm going to turn it into a parking lot!" he said. "I'll cut down that big tree, pave it over, and charge people to park here!"

"Cut down the tree!" cried Holly.

"I don't think we need a parking lot in this neighborhood," said Amelia Bedelia. "There's plenty of room already for people to park their cars."

"And lots of people walk," Heather pointed out.

"Or ride bikes," said Holly.

"And fall off them," added Amelia Bedelia.

"Maybe your parents are looking for you girls," said Victor Lee.

"It'll be *perfect*!" shouted the man in the parrot shirt. "I'll charge people to park their cars by the hour, by the day, by the week, by the month. I'll clean up!"

"But we already cleaned up!" Amelia Bedelia exclaimed. "We worked really hard!"

The man in the parrot shirt was not listening. He was grinning, and he got into the car with Victor Lee, still talking about how much money he would make.

Chapter 9
Minsk and Timbuktu

"What's wrong, sweetie?" Amelia Bedelia's mother asked her that night at dinner. "You look pretty blue."

Amelia Bedelia looked down at her shirt. "I am totally pink," she said. "Except for my red tie-dyed heart."

"Pink looks good," said her mother. "But you look sad. Is something wrong?"

Amelia Bedelia nodded and poked her kale. She told her parents about Mr. Lee finding a buyer for the lot.

"Honey, that's a shame," said her mother. "After all your hard work—our hard work! I can tell you're disappointed."

Her parents exchanged a look in parent code. Her mother tipped her head to one side. Her father's eyebrows moved closer together. It was a look that said, "We're worried about our daughter."

If Amelia Bedelia's parents had been using words, not code, they would have said, "What's happened to Amelia Bedelia? Why isn't she talking a mile a

minute? Why isn't she waving her arms around so fast that kale flies off her fork? Why is she . . . quiet?"

She looked worse than disappointed. She looked discouraged. That was not like Amelia Bedelia at all.

"I just don't see how we can be an explorers' club anymore," Amelia Bedelia said with a sigh. "We needed a cool place to meet. Somewhere different. Somewhere exciting. Somewhere like a tree house. How can we go on adventures if the only place we have to meet is in our own backyards?"

"Your own backyard?" said her father. "I remember when there was a zoo in your very own backyard!"

93

Amelia Bedelia smiled a tiny smile. Her zoo had had a big cat sitting on a fluffy pillow, a frozen gecko in a block of ice, and a genuine monkey. All the neighborhood kids had come. Even her teacher had shown up!

"You of all people don't need a tree house to have adventures," said her mother. "Remember when you rode your bike in the parade? And got chased by all the dogs in town, who wanted to eat up your lemon tarts? And you won a new bike because of it? Now that was an adventure!"

"You'll always be an explorer, Amelia Bedelia," her dad promised her. "You can have adventures right here at home, as long as you're willing to try new things."

"Like kale?" asked Amelia Bedelia, looking down at her plate. She was starting to feel a little better.

"Well . . ." said her father.

Her mom reached over and lifted Amelia Bedelia's plate right off the table.

"You know what?" she said. "I don't think this is a kale day. I think it's a day for tomato salad instead."

After dinner, the phone rang. "Amelia Bedelia!" her mom called. "It's for you!"

"Hi, Amelia Bedelia," said the voice on the other end of the phone. "This is Jill. We met at Pete's Diner the other day. Do you remember?"

"Sure," said Amelia Bedelia.

"Well, I heard something through the

RING RING RING

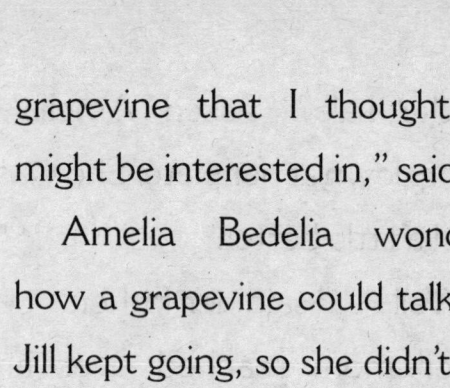

grapevine that I thought you might be interested in," said Jill.

Amelia Bedelia wondered how a grapevine could talk. But Jill kept going, so she didn't have a chance to ask.

"The owner of the lot is named Mrs. West, and she lives right next door to it, in a gray three-story house with a big porch out front. You know the one I mean?"

Yes, Amelia Bedelia knew just which one Jill meant. It was the spooky house where she'd had the sense that somebody was watching them from behind the curtains.

"I know Mrs. West—she gives talks at the library sometimes and she's wonderful. Maybe if you spoke to her, she'd wait for a while before selling the lot."

"I don't think so," said Amelia Bedelia with a sigh. She told Jill about Victor Lee and the man who had been so excited about building a parking lot.

"Gee, that's too bad," said Jill. "I'm sorry, Amelia Bedelia. I can tell this means a lot to you."

But Amelia Bedelia couldn't help thinking more about Jill's idea as she got ready for bed. There was a chance, wasn't there, that Mrs. West might change her mind? She should at least try to talk to her. Wasn't that what an adventurer would do?

The next day Amelia Bedelia, Heather, and Holly had a quick club meeting on

Amelia Bedelia's front porch.

"Oh, I don't know, Amelia Bedelia," said Holly. "Will Mrs. West really listen to us? She doesn't even know us, and we're just kids."

"We should try!" insisted Heather. "We're explorers, aren't we?"

"That's right!" said Amelia Bedelia. "And explorers don't give up and turn

back just because their boots start to leak or they run out of food."

"Or the river floods and washes away their jeep," Heather added.

"Or piranhas eat their map," said Amelia Bedelia.

"Or piranhas eat the explorers!" Heather finished.

"Okay! Okay!" said Holly. "I'll come. But I bet Mrs. West won't care about what we think."

"We should probably ask our parents first," said Heather. And that's what they did!

The next day the three friends met at the lot and climbed up the steps of Mrs. West's front porch.

The house still looked a bit spooky to Amelia Bedelia. Not that she believed in ghosts. Or zombies. Or vampires. Or zombie vampire bats with sharp fangs that might swoop down on them from the attic. But still, if she were making a movie about a haunted house, the haunted house would look just like this one.

The porch steps creaked. The doorbell wheezed and sighed instead of ringing.

The door opened slowly.

"Oh, my," said the lady who looked at them through the doorway. She had short white hair, bright purple glasses, and a wide smile. "You're the girls who have been cleaning up my empty lot, aren't you? You did a wonderful job. I wanted to go out

and thank you, but I sprained my ankle in the garden last week, and I haven't been able to walk very well. You haven't seen a cat, have you? Or two?"

"We saw a gray cat in a bush when we were cleaning up," said Heather.

"And we saw a black cat in a tree yesterday," said Holly.

"Those are mine!" said Mrs. West. "The gray one is Timbuktu and the black

one is Minsk. They haven't come in for their food, and that's not like them. I'm a bit worried. But I've forgotten my manners! Come in, girls, come in."

Leaning on a cane, Mrs. West ushered the girls into a wide front hallway. "Wow!" said Amelia Bedelia, looking around.

"Zowie!" added Heather.

"Yikes!" said Holly.

There was a beautiful rug with tassels on the floor. A mirror, whose frame had been carved with hundreds of tiny flowers, hung on one wall. Amelia Bedelia could see pictures of the pyramids of Egypt and the Eiffel Tower and a huge red rock sticking up out of flat desert land. She saw photos

of tall churches built of stone, and a city that seemed to have rivers instead of streets, and a marketplace where stalls were heaped with golden marigolds and women wore saris as bright as the flowers. She saw monkeys swinging through tall green trees, and giraffes ambling across grassy plains, and penguins sliding across slippery ice.

"Now, what can I do for you girls?" asked Mrs. West. "Besides saying thank you for such a lot of work."

"Maybe we can do something for you first," said Amelia Bedelia. "Can we help find your cats?"

"That would be wonderful!" said Mrs. West. "I'm worried they might

have gotten up into the attic. My ankle is still bothering me, and the attic stairs are quite steep. I don't think I could climb them. Would you mind checking?"

"We don't mind," said Amelia Bedelia.

Mrs. West showed them the way up to the second floor. There was a huge wooden horn hanging on the wall above the staircase. Amelia Bedelia ran her fingers along it as they climbed.

"Here's the door to the attic," Mrs. West said.

The door was a little bit open. Amelia Bedelia pushed it open all the way and looked up a narrow, dusty flight of stairs.

She could see two trails of little paw prints in the dust. It looked like the cats

really had gone this way.

But the stairs looked rickety . . . and kind of spooky.

Amelia Bedelia wanted to help Mrs. West. Her mother had remembered that Mrs. West used to take classes at the yoga studio and that she was funny and interesting. Amelia Bedelia wanted to find Timbuktu and Minsk. She didn't want to be a scaredy-cat. For a moment she imagined herself with whiskers and pointy ears, cowering under a bed.

No, that wasn't how an explorer acted. If two real cats could go up into that creepy attic, couldn't an adventurer like Amelia Bedelia follow them?

Chapter 10

A New Explorer

"You go first, Amelia Bedelia," Holly said, peering up the attic stairs over Amelia Bedelia's shoulder.

"Why me?" asked Amelia Bedelia.

"You're president today," said Holly.

"I am?" asked Amelia Bedelia.

"Sure," Heather said nervously.

Amelia Bedelia sighed. If she was

president of an explorers' club, she really had no choice.

"Here, Timbuktu! Here, Minsk!" she called as she climbed up the creaky stairs.

At the top, she stepped out into a wide, dusty space. And she screamed.

Actually, it came out as a squeak. A huge face with dark, scary eyes and a long, skinny nose was laughing at her from the far wall.

Holly yelped—before all three girls realized that what they were looking at was a wooden mask.

"Oh, gosh," said Holly. "My heart's in my mouth!"

Amelia Bedelia's heart was where it usually was . . . but it was thumping.

There were lots of old trunks in the attic, and piles of boxes. Cobwebs swung from the rafters overhead.

Amelia Bedelia followed the paw prints, trying not to think of ghosts or goblins or vampire bats. Or vampire cats!

Something brushed the top of Amelia Bedelia's hair, like a ghostly hand. She squeaked again, and Heather grabbed her shoulder.

Amelia Bedelia looked up. A kite with a long, dangling tail hung from the ceiling. A fierce face with a scowling mouth was painted on it.

"Yikes!" whispered Holly.

But Amelia Bedelia was starting to feel braver. A kite and a mask and cobwebs and shadows were not enough to stop true explorers! She tiptoed past a bucket. She saw more pails and buckets in other spots around the attic. She looked up. There were holes in the roof.

The paw print trail led across the attic to a half-open window. There were more paw prints on the sill.

"I bet the cats went out the window!" Holly said.

"I'm sure they did," said Amelia Bedelia.

"How can you be so sure?" asked Heather.

Amelia Bedelia pointed. "Because I see them over there," she said.

The three girls crowded around the window and looked out.

Next to Mrs. West's house was a smaller building. As they watched, the girls saw a fluffy gray shape leap across the gap between the house and the smaller building and land on the roof. A sleek black shape was already there, waiting.

The two cats walked across the roof of the other building and disappeared.

"The cat's out of the bag!" said Holly, and giggled.

"I think both cats are out of the attic," said Amelia Bedelia.

"I meant, now we know the secret of where the cats are," said Holly. "Let's tell Mrs. West!"

"The carriage house!" exclaimed Mrs. West when the girls told her what they had seen. "Oh, thank you, girls! I never would have thought to check there. Follow me!"

The girls followed Mrs. West outside and into the other building. Amelia Bedelia

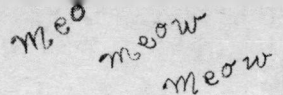

looked around, but to her surprise, she didn't see any carriages. Just two very old-looking cars.

Soft meows came from a loft overhead. "That's where those cats are!" said Mrs. West, shaking her head. "How will we ever get them to come down?"

There was a ladder leading up to the loft. "We could climb up," said Holly.

"But could we climb down while we're holding cats?" asked Heather.

"I have a better idea!" Amelia Bedelia

112

said. "Do you have any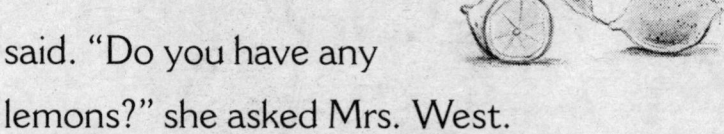
lemons?" she asked Mrs. West.

Mrs. West did have lemons. Better than that, she had lemon marmalade and sugar cookies. Amelia Bedelia spread a little marmalade on a cookie and left it at the foot of the ladder. Then the three girls and Mrs. West waited.

"Wow," said Heather. "Look at these cars. They look old!"

"Just like me," Mrs. West agreed.

One of the cars was a convertible, silver and sleek and curvy. It looked almost as if it would float or fly as well as it could drive. The other car was square and boxy, with big spoked wheels and a steering wheel on a stick.

"My husband loved old cars," said Mrs. West. "These were the last two in his collection. Nobody else in my family has room to keep them. I've been trying to sell them, but it takes such a long time to find the right buyer for cars like these. They're white elephants, really."

Amelia Bedelia looked hard at the cars, but she could not see any long dangling trunks or big floppy ears.

Just then there was a quiet meow from the top of the ladder, and a black, whiskered face poked out of the loft.

"That's Minsk!" whispered Mrs. West.

Slowly, rung by rung, Minsk eased himself down the ladder until he could start licking the marmalade off the cookie.

The gray, fluffy cat appeared and meowed. "Timbuktu!" Mrs. West said.

Timbuktu scampered down the ladder and pushed Minsk aside so that she could also have a bite of lemon marmalade.

"Thank goodness!" said Mrs. West. She scooped up Minsk. Amelia Bedelia picked up Timbuktu. "Bring her inside, would you?" asked

Mrs. West. "Then I can pour you some lemonade to thank you for your help!"

They carried the cats back into the house. Amelia Bedelia paused in the front hallway to look again at the pictures on the wall. One in particular caught her eye. In it, a woman was standing on the edge of an enormous canyon, waving. She had glasses and short hair and she looked a lot like . . .

"That's you!" said Amelia Bedelia.

"Yes, it is!" Mrs. West smiled even more widely. "Good eye. My husband took those pictures. He was a wonderful photographer."

"Have you really been to all these places?" Amelia Bedelia asked.

"Certainly," said Mrs. West. "When I was a bit younger, of course. My husband and I loved to travel together."

"Wow," said Amelia Bedelia again. "You must have been around the world!"

Mrs. West laughed. "More than once!" she said. "But come into the kitchen, girls. I'll feed these silly cats and pour you some lemonade, and you can tell me what you wanted to see me about."

Chapter 11

Another Woman's Treasure

Mrs. West poured tall glasses of icy lemonade and set out sugar cookies. "First, tell me how you knew my cats would like lemon marmalade," she said.

"Because we knew that Minsk, at least, likes lemon tarts!" said Amelia Bedelia. She explained how she had coaxed Minsk down out of a tree with one of her tarts.

Then the girls told Mrs. West about their club, and how a tree house would be a perfect meeting place, and how the oak tree in her lot would be the perfect place for that tree house.

"So we were wondering . . . maybe . . ." Amelia Bedelia said. "Could you *not* sell the lot after all?"

"Oh, dear." Mrs. West sighed. "I'm sorry, girls, but the truth is, I need the money. I want to stay in this house as long as I can. It's full of wonderful memories and all the things my husband and I collected in our travels. But the roof has started to leak, and I need to repair it quickly. There are some other things around the house that need work also.

That's why I decided to sell the lot."

Amelia Bedelia felt terrible.

"It's a shame." Mrs. West finished up her glass of lemonade. "I wish I could help out three fellow explorers. Would you like to see some things we collected on our travels? I imagine you saw my mask from Nigeria up in the attic, and the kite from Japan too. There are some other interesting mementoes I could show you."

"I'd love to see them," said Heather.

"Yes, please!" said Holly.

Amelia Bedelia was not sure. "Did you really bring home toes?" she asked. "And just men's toes, or are there any from women?"

Mrs. West laughed. "'Mementoes'

is another word for souvenirs. Things that I've collected from all over."

"In that case," said Amelia Bedelia, "I'd love to see them too."

Mrs. West told them that the wooden horn hanging above the staircase was a didgeridoo from Australia. There were swords from Spain hanging in the library, and a fan made of peacock feathers on a desk. Next to the fan was a jar full of coins from countries all over the world,

and also a giant shell, shiny pink inside, that Mrs. West had found in Bermuda. When Amelia Bedelia held it up to her ear, she could hear the sea.

"I'm sorry that I couldn't help with your tree house," Mrs. West told them when it was time for them to leave. "Do come back another day. I love having company."

The three friends headed home. Amelia Bedelia took a last look at Mrs. West's house as they walked down the block. It did not look spooky to her anymore. It looked like a house full of treasures, like a wonderful place to explore.

"That was exciting!" said Holly. "I loved that long horn thing the best. What did Mrs. West call it?"

"A didgeridoo," said Heather.

"Is there a didgeridon't?" asked Amelia Bedelia.

"I liked the kite in the attic," said Holly.

"I liked all of it," said Amelia Bedelia. "I understand why Mrs. West wants to stay in her house, with all those cool souvenirs and mementoes. But I wish there was some way we could have the tree house

and Mrs. West could have the money she needs to fix up her home at the same time!"

That night Amelia Bedelia perched on a stool in the kitchen, tearing up lettuce for a salad and telling her parents all about her visit to Mrs. West's house. She described the photographs, the kite, the swords, the didgeridoo, and finally the cars in the garage.

"They're really neat," she said, dumping the lettuce into a bowl. "But Mrs. West says nobody in her family wants them."

"Can you toss the salad, Amelia Bedelia?" asked her father.

Amelia Bedelia picked up the bowl of salad and eyed the ceiling. "How high?" she asked.

"I mean, put some dressing on it and use the tongs to gently shake things around so the dressing gets on every vegetable," said her father. "And about the cars, just remember—one man's trash is another man's treasure."

"The cars are not treasure," said Amelia Bedelia. "And they are not carriages or elephants either. They're just cars, but pretty cool old ones. Plus, they belong to Mrs. West, and she is a woman, not a man."

"Some cars can be treasure," her father explained. "Valuable. Worth a lot of money."

"How much money?" asked Amelia Bedelia.

"No idea," said her father. "I don't know that much about old cars."

"But I bet your friend Wild Bill does," said her mother. "Why don't you ask him?"

The next morning Amelia Bedelia woke up to the sound of leaves brushing against her window. The wind had picked up, and the trees were dancing.

Something inside Amelia Bedelia was dancing too—excitement! She dialed Wild Bill's number, thinking about those cool old cars in Mrs. West's carriage house. Her dad had said cars could be treasures, hadn't he? And Mrs. West needed money, didn't she? What if those old cars really were valuable? Maybe Mrs. West would

126

not have to sell the lot! Maybe there was a tree house in Amelia Bedelia's future, after all!

"Howdy!" said a voice on the phone. "Thank you for calling Wild Bill's Auto-Rama, the home of the sweet deal! Are you in the market for a new car today?"

"Actually, no," said Amelia Bedelia. "I'm at home."

"I know who this is," said Wild Bill. "Amelia Bedelia, right?"

"That's right," said Amelia Bedelia. "And I have a question for you. I know someone who has two cars. Old ones. I was wondering if they might be worth a lot of money."

"Lots of people have old cars in their

garages, little lady," said Wild Bill. "And usually they're not worth one red cent."

"I don't think these would be worth one cent, no matter what color it is," Amelia Bedelia agreed. "I think they might be worth lots of dollars. One of them looks really old. It has a steering wheel on a stick. And the other one is silver and curvy and shiny. On the front it says something that starts with an F. Furry . . . no, Ferrari."

"What? What? What?" shouted Wild Bill into the phone.

"Ferrari!" Amelia Bedelia shouted back.

"Little lady, meet me right away at your friend's house! Tell me where it is!" Wild Bill exclaimed. "And hold on to your hat! This could be very exciting!"

Amelia Bedelia told her parents where she was going and hurried over to Mrs. West's. The wind whistled past her ears and tugged at her baseball cap.

When she got there, Wild Bill was waiting by the carriage house with Mrs. West. Amelia Bedelia waved to them and clamped her hands together on the top of her head.

"What are you doing?" Wild Bill asked.

"I'm hanging on to my hat, like you said," Amelia Bedelia explained. "Or else the wind might blow it away." She looked up at him. "Or I guess you might eat it."

"Ma'am, can we see those cars?" Wild Bill asked

Mrs. West. "I was happy to wait for this little lady, but I tell you, I'm so excited I've got ants in my pants!"

Amelia Bedelia took a step back. "How did they get in there?" she asked.

Smiling, Mrs. West unlocked the carriage house door.

"Jumping Jehoshaphat!" Wild Bill exclaimed. "I don't believe it!"

He ran into the carriage house. He circled around the cars. He peered underneath them. He peeked under the hoods. He was beaming.

"Ma'am," he said to Mrs. West, "I'd be very honored to sell these cars for you."

"Well!" Mrs. West was smiling too. "I can hardly believe it! Perhaps they'll bring in enough to let me make the repairs my house needs. What a windfall!"

"Did you fall?" asked Amelia Bedelia, concerned. "Did the wind push you over?"

"No," said Mrs. West, laughing. "This is just the best news I've had in a long time—all thanks to you, Amelia Bedelia!"

That night, before dinner, the phone rang. It was Mrs. West. "Guess what,

Amelia Bedelia?" she said. "Your friend Wild Bill found a buyer for my cars right away. With the money from the sale, I'll be able to make my repairs."

"That's great," said Amelia Bedelia.

"So I don't have to sell my lot," Mrs. West went on. "In fact, I've decided to donate that land to the community to be made into a park."

"That's really great!" said Amelia Bedelia. "A park to play in is way better than a place to park cars!"

Chapter 12

Here's to
Amelia Bedelia!

One bright and sunny morning not too long after Mrs. West sold her cars, Amelia Bedelia jumped out of bed and did a little dance with Finally. The big day was here at last. She could hardly wait!

First, Heather and Holly and

their parents drove to Amelia Bedelia's house. The girls were so excited that they skipped and ran and turned cartwheels in the yard while the grown-ups talked.

But finally everybody was ready. The girls jumped on their bikes. The moms and dads walked behind. Amelia Bedelia's mom carried a large white box, and her dad held Finally's leash.

Amelia Bedelia felt easy and breezy, zipping along. She led the way right to the empty lot next to Mrs. West's house. Only it wasn't an empty lot anymore.

Today was the new park's opening day!

Amelia Bedelia braked her bike and coasted to a stop. Heather and Holly were right behind her.

"Wow," Holly whispered.

"Amazing!" Heather added. "I didn't think it would be this good!"

"I did," said Amelia Bedelia, looking around with a satisfied smile. "I knew it would be the best park in town!"

It was a park made for adventures. There were curving, swooping lanes for riding bikes. There was a wall to practice rock climbing. There were nets and ladders made of rope to clamber up and long, long ropes to swing on. There was

a fountain kids could splash in. And best of all, there was—

"Our tree house!" Holly exclaimed.

It was the best tree house in the world. Amelia Bedelia was sure of it. It had everything the girls had talked about: a rope ladder, a hammock, a telescope,

and two ways to get down—a slide and a pole. It was the perfect place for an explorers' club to meet.

A little black dog with long legs came dashing up to sniff Finally. Diana came running after her. "Sorry!" she gasped. "Licorice is very excited about this new park!"

"We are too!" said Amelia Bedelia.

Everyone in the neighborhood was excited. The park was full of parents and kids. Pete was trying out the climbing wall. Doris was cheering him on. Amelia Bedelia waved at her friend Charlie, who was chasing his poodle, Pierre, through the fountain. Mrs. West was sitting on a

bench, looking around with a wide smile, and Wild Bill was at her side.

"Here you go, Amelia Bedelia," said her mother, handing her the large white box.

Amelia Bedelia took the box and brought it over to Wild Bill.

"Howdy!" said Wild Bill. Mrs. West gave Amelia Bedelia a kiss on the cheek.

"Howdy!" Amelia Bedelia said back. "I brought something for you!" And she handed the box to Wild Bill.

"For me?" Wild Bill looked surprised.

He opened the box carefully. First he smiled. Then he started to laugh out loud.

"Look what this little lady has done in her kitchen!" he chortled.

Inside the box was a cake in the shape of a hat—a ten-gallon cowboy hat.

"You said you'd eat your hat if we cleaned up this lot and got a tree house here," said Amelia Bedelia. "And we did!"

Amelia Bedelia's parents had forks and paper plates too. Wild Bill served pieces of his cake hat, chuckling all the while.

"A toast!" he said, holding up a piece of cake on a fork.

"No, it's cake," said Amelia Bedelia.

"Chocolate with marshmallow frosting."

Wild Bill shook his head. "A toast means that we honor somebody who has done something extraordinary," he said. "And this toast is for you. To Miss Amelia Bedelia and her friends! They did a lot to make this new park happen!"

"To Amelia Bedelia and her friends!" everyone in the park called out, and Amelia Bedelia blushed.

Amelia Bedelia and Heather and Holly sat down on the bench beside Mrs. West to eat cake and watch people enjoying the park. "We want to ask you something," said Heather to Mrs. West.

"And tell you something," Amelia Bedelia added.

"Go right ahead!" Mrs. West said cheerfully.

"We found a name for our club at last," said Amelia Bedelia. "We are going to be the Easy Breezy East and West Explorers' Club!"

"Perfect," said Mrs. West, smiling. "And what did you want to ask?"

"Will you be in the club too?" Holly asked. "You're the best explorer we know."

"I'd be honored," Mrs. West answered.

"We'll meet in the tree house in the summer," said Holly.

"And in the winter we can meet in my house!" said Mrs. West.

"Will you tell us some more about your adventures?" asked Heather.

"I certainly will," said Mrs. West. "And we will all follow the first and only rule of the Easy Breezy East and West Explorers' Club . . ."

"No being bored!" all four explorers shouted together.

"Explorers rule!" added Amelia Bedelia.

Two Ways to Say It

By Amelia Bedelia

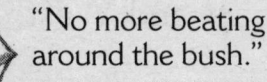

"No more beating around the bush."

"Stop wasting time."

"It's an eyesore."

"It's really ugly."

"The cat's out of the bag!"

"Everyone knows the secret!"

"I'll eat my hat!"

"I'll be super surprised!"

"My name will be mud!"

"I'll be in big trouble!"

144

"You're barking up the
wrong tree."

"You are totally wrong."

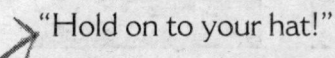

"You're a million
miles away."

"You aren't paying
attention."

"Hold on to your hat!"

"It's going to get
exciting!"

"You girls really
got the rug pulled
out from under you."

"I'm so excited I've got
ants in my pants!"

"Someone upset
your plans."

"I'm so excited
I can't stand still!"

The Amelia Bedelia Chapter Books
Have you read them all?

Coming
soon!

Coming
soon!

Amelia Bedelia wants a new bike—a brand-new shiny, beautiful, fast bike just like Suzanne's new bike. Amelia Bedelia's dad says that a bike like that is really expensive and will cost an arm and a leg. Amelia Bedelia doesn't want to give away one of her arms and one of her legs. She'll need both arms to steer her new bike, and both legs to pedal it.

Amelia Bedelia is going to get a puppy—a sweet, adorable, loyal, friendly puppy! When Amelia Bedelia's parents ask her what kind of dog she'd like, Amelia Bedelia doesn't know what to say. There are hundreds and thousands of dogs in the world, maybe even millions!

Amelia Bedelia is hitting the road. Where is she going? It's a surprise! But one thing is certain. Amelia Bedelia and her mom and dad will try new things (like fishing), they'll eat a lot of pizza (yum), and Amelia Bedelia will meet a new friend—a friend she'll never, *ever* forget.

Amelia Bedelia has an amazing idea! She is going to design and build a zoo in her backyard. Better yet, she is going to invite all her friends to bring their pets and help plan the exhibits and rides.

Amelia Bedelia usually loves recess. One day, though, she doesn't get picked for a team and she begins to have second thoughts about sports. What's so great about racing and jumping and catching, anyway?

#7 Coming soon!

Time for vacation! Amelia Bedelia is having fun with her cousin at the beach. But who is that kid they see everywhere they go?

#8 Coming soon!

Amelia Bedelia loves to dance, but she's not sure ballet is for her. Everyone pitches in to help her keep her toes tapping, in this silly story about dancing and performing on the big stage.

If you were going to explore the world, where would you go?

Amelia Bedelia dreams of exploring . . .

- The Great Sphinx in Egypt

- The Mayan pyramids in Central America

 • The rain forest

- The streets of Rome